Tao of Life and Death

A Tale

Dedicated to Dad & Mom

ISBN: 1469924056 ISBN-13: 9781469924052

5

CHINA
Ming Dynasty
1368-1644

Beijing

Yellow River

Luoyang

Xian

Nanjing

Chengdu

Yangtze River

Guangzhou

Hainan Island

CHINA

Luoyang
Henan Province
CHINA

HENAN
PROVINCE
- CHINA -

Luoyang

Longmen
Grottoes

△ Song Mountain
Shaolin Temple

NARRATORS

Gnarled Pine
Taoist Hermit

Happy Willow
Boy, Scholar

Zhong Kui

Quiet Buffalo
Taoist Master

Stephen
Author & Artist

Foreword

My image appears at the beginning and end of this book. But I am conscience within every drop of ink and woven into each fiber of paper in between. I am the shadow behind every lotus bloom. To demons and ghosts, I am vengeance's doom. Read on and follow the way, for I am the guardian of this tale.

—Zhong Kui

Zhong Kui

Chapter One

Gnarled Pine
Taoist Hermit

Turtle, tiger, man transformed,
Three in one, spirit forms.
Longevity, might, flesh,
Follow the way to escape death.
Taoist hermit in mountains, I stride
In tune with nature, staff by my side.

Crane, goose, badger, bear,
Duck, snake, deer, hare,
Monkey, cricket, horse, cat,
Elephant, toad, dog, bat.
All are my companions, one by one,
We share life under the rising and setting sun.

Sit and listen to the story I give,
And you may learn how to live.
Day turns night, then day again,
Oh, how wheels of life do spin.

13

Learn now, later; I don't mind.
I am known as Gnarled Pine.

Long ago there lived a man named Zhong Kui (Jong Koo-way). He was a talented, bright man, who had set his eyes upon officialdom. He dreamt of placing first in the imperial exam, and nothing less would suit his plan. He had proven his immense ability in the local and provincial tests, but only after the imperial exam would he be able to rest. Through the examination system one could find fame, status, honor, and wealth—prizes rightly won, but rarely dealt.

But as a poor scholar in the far reaches of Western China, in order to take the imperial exam Zhong Kui would need money and gifts for the long trip to the capital city. Where would one turn to find such funds? A rich benefactor should have the sum! So he introduced himself to a suitor who could provide him with money and a gift to ward off looters. The benefactor gave him a sword for protection's sake, for the roads had many bandits and coins and life might they take.

So, leaving his sister and mother behind, off Zhong Kui went, accompanied by his loyal friend Du Ping. They made good time. One day as light began to dim, they spied a Buddhist temple and stopped; it was a good place to rest—or so they thought. On learning of Zhong Kui's mission, the monks threw him a huge feast to celebrate his quest and wished good tidings for their honored guest. They prayed for the luck that Buddha would bring. Chanting, rhythmic prayers they did sing. Then Zhong Kui, with too much drink and attitude, became brash and ill of mood. With each cup of wine, he would boast. Tossing about self-compliments, he did toast. The monks took notice of his self-given pride and told him to keep it inside. They said, "We threw this feast to honor Buddha and pray for your good luck, not to hear you cluck, cluck, cluck." On hearing this admonishment, Zhong Kui took great offense. With vigor he drew his sword and cursed with many foul words. It was this he spat out:

14

If you call upon Buddha to bless my fate,
You waste your words and rouse my hate.
You should pray to get rid of the Buddha himself,
Hear my words, you monkeys, so my judgment is felt.
I go to the capital to make my life better,
In this temple, your lives do you slowly fritter.
Your chants are just words lost in the wind,
You imprison yourselves here for fear of sin.
I spit my wine into your face,
You idle your lives believing in faith.
Why don't you do something but worship?
Do you not have some earthly purpose?
Plow a field, shape some wood,
Do something—something! If only you could.
I need no prayers to Buddha or gods,
Your prattling doth not increase my odds.
I'll pass the test as the hawk doth fly,
If not, so do I hope to die.

There was not much to say or feast about after that. The words were out, the dice were cast. Was it the wine that turned the hour sour? Too much pride? Too much self? For the way Zhong Kui treated these brothers, surely he would treat others. For men they were, as was he; for careless words become karma's deeds. He himself did anger spew, loosened by the coaxing brew. The tame tongue can slip its noose when judgment wanes. Liquid enticement can unleash words that should remain restrained. Soon everyone retired for the evening; but meddlesome, devilish demons took note of the words Zhong Kui had spoken.

Who was this man who chastised monks and wished Buddha gone? Who was this man who ruined a feast and did others wrong? The demons conspired to egg him on: "Let's stoke his coals and feed his hate; as a tool of ours he will slay these monks as he did scorn their faith. Let his wrath and anger serve our purpose in disguise. If he believes they have done him wrong, then they will not survive. Let's change his appearance

15

this very night so in the morn he will strike, and thereby do our deeds wrongly right."

During the dark of that drunken eve, the demons changed Zhong Kui's appearance to ugliness for all to see. They cast a spell with a magical green mist that once inhaled would do its bit. As a waning moon shed meager light, crickets chirped and toads croaked. Zhong Kui snored and sucked the mist down his throat. When dawn broke bright, Zhong Kui rose with a face for fright. Tiger eyes now bulged from his head, while his belly was round as if overfed. His hair and beard had grown out like wild weeds, while his arms and legs had become thick and strong like the trunks of trees. His friend, Du Ping, was shocked by this sudden new view, and he could only guess that this was Zhong Kui, the man he knew.

Du Ping spoke. "Zhong Kui, is that you?"

Zhong Kui grumbled back, "Of course it's me. Can't you see? I'm off to breakfast to feed my hunger, but first I must wash from my face my drunken slumber."

While he bent over the water, a liquid mirror-filled basin, shock overtook him at what he was facing. He stumbled back and mumbled, "Is that me? Oh, I can't believe...doth this reflection deceive?" He peeked again and stammered out loud, "What happened to my figure and face? What spell of magic did these monks on me place? He thought, I must rid myself of this temple's gloom. I fear that this may forecast doom. It seems some Buddhist charm or chant has changed my looks. Damn these monks, these devilish crooks. From the seeds of offense I sowed last night have I reaped this lot; my very own tongue has brought what I have got. I have no heart to settle this score, for my fate I must pursue no matter the obstacles in store. "Du Ping, we have no time to waste, we must be off at a quickened pace. We have just enough time if we move with purpose. These monks prayed for our luck, but I fear in fact they did curse us."

16

So off they went on their mission to find success. The demons were wrong in what they guessed. Zhong Kui was not evil like them, but actually had goodness within. While his outward demeanor had been rough and gruff, his inside was made of finer stuff. Once the wine had run its course, he remembered his duty's course. He had no vengeance in his heart, only the purpose for which his journey did start.

Chapter Two

Gnarled Pine
Taoist Hermit

The streets of the capital city bustled with life. Zhong Kui and Du Ping eagerly searched for an inn before the embrace of night. At the Plum Blossom Inn they found food, shelter, and rest—a reprieve, for the moment, from the oncoming test.

Zhong Kui and Du Ping supped together in their dank room. Zhong Kui's eyelids grew heavy, due to meat and wine consumed. He lay down in bed, drifting off to sleep, and soon into his mind a dream did creep. He had a premonition of troubling sorrow, perhaps an ill-boding sign of tomorrow.

Zhong Kui dreamt…
Two fish swim in a pond;
Of each other are they fond.
Each of the same mother:
One sister, one brother.

19

One red, one gold,
First shy, second bold.
The male fish into a dragon turns,
Now for a prized pearl he yearns.

Shape of snake;
Tail and scales of fish;
Antlers of stag;
Face of camel;
Feet of tiger;
Talons of eagle;
Eyes of demon;
Blue of hue;
Infinite of strength—
Off into the sky he flew.

He chased a precious flaming pearl in gleeful rapture,
But no matter how fast he flew, it could not be captured.
Then from down below, a man to his soldiers yelled,
"Send that beast back to hell!
Shoot, shoot, shoot your arrows!
Ward off this monster that chills my marrow."

The dragon replied from up on high,
"Fear me not; I mean no harm,
You need not cause such alarm."

An arrow then struck true into the dragon's heart,
And from his lips these words did part...

"Why do you fear the sight of me?
Am I not life, as are thee?
I only sought what belonged to me."

The dragon then fell like a drop of rain,

All the while in anguished pain.
Cold he grew, by rushing wind,
His once-warmed blood chilled within.

His mind drifted back to the secluded pond.
Had ambition steered him wrong?
No more time to ponder why.
Regrets in life rarely die.
Drifting fast to hardened earth,
Death ends a life that began with birth.
Like a heavy flake of snow,
Said dragon braced for the final blow.

Now as Zhong Kui dreamt, his blood grew cold in his veins, and icy sweat poured from his mighty frame. Wet, weak, and shivering cold, he awoke and gasped for air as if being choked. "Where am I? Where am I?"

Then, finding composure, Zhong Kui began to calm. He realized he was free of any real harm. He rationalized that what seemed real was only a silly, never-mind dream. He even broke into a soliloquy:

A mere figment of my imagination,
An inconsequential cognition,
An irrelevant musing,
A frivolous moment of fancy,
A nonessential impression,
A paltry thought to be given no time.

Thereby, Zhong Kui pushed the nightmare from his mind and thought of the exam for which he pined. His entire chi was focused for the test. He yearned to prove that he was the best.

In the morning, Zhong Kui arrived at the palace, and he was indeed a brutish sight. Others avoided him as if scared of blight. The examination officials and fellow candidates took more than a glance at his forbidding

21

condition, and his appearance could not help but arouse suspicion. Whirling, dancing murmurs flew about, but Zhong Kui focused from within—and blocked the without. In an almost trancelike state, he channeled his brain, for the test of all tests was about to begin. Zhong Kui sat down at his allotted spot, vowing to himself to come out on top.

"Silence!" the head official yelled. The room hushed as noise fell. Paper, ink, and calligraphy brushes were distributed to the men. They all felt anxious for the exam to finally begin. Tension was high in the stagnant air; some had faith and others, despair. "Go!" the head official yelled. Five of fifty fainted, as if dealt a knockout blow. One man's heart exploded from the exciting start—the race was off as from life he did part. Zhong Kui's brush moved to the rhythm of his thoughts, and clever were the answers his brilliance brought. He had mastered the teachings of Confucius and Mencius, the knowledge of the spring and autumn annals, and many a poem (a few even his own). Zhong Kui produced elegant sentences like an unbroken chain. He poured out all of his talent; from giving his last ounce, he did not refrain. Never happier had Zhong Kui been; he rejoiced in silence, and swelled proudly within. He had met the moment and flown to heights where only dragons dared. Tomorrow he would see how he had fared.

"Stop!" screamed the head official. "Put your brush down." The weight of the moment had been dispelled, and the men thanked God, as if freed from hell. The task, once ripe green, was now as a brown, withered leaf. What had begun with high anxiety ended with great relief.

The papers were gathered for grading, and the joy of the short-lived reprieve soon began to fade. Now objective and subjective opinion would be applied. Would these scholars see the results for which they had vied? Their futures lay inside testing scrolls, a manifestation of their very souls. Some would find the light of sweet success, while others would experience dark pangs of regret.

The examination officials shuffled off to a secluded place and recopied the exams so they would not know which test matched which face. They studied and pondered the depth of each line and took into account the poetic styling of the author's mind. A passing or failing grade was then affixed, and soon these results would determine how each scholar would hereupon exist.

The next morning, the official exam results were posted on the palace gates. The candidates craned their necks about, searching for their fate. One by one, they celebrated or sulked; some found joy, while others found fault. Zhong Kui shoved himself in and searched, name by name; oh, the anxiety and excitement built up to a heavy strain. His hopes had risen to such a high degree that he uttered out loud, "My name! My name! Where art thou?" Then, at the bottom of the list, he found his name—last in order but first in place! He let out a shout of excitement and embraced Du Ping. He relished the thoughts of what his success would bring. He would acquire an official title, grand salary, and lofty position. He could take care of his family and make important decisions. His future was as bright as the noonday sun. He had chased his dream and fairly won.

The emperor himself would award the successful candidates the next day—the event Zhong Kui had dreamed of was coming his way. Everyone celebrated with wine, food, and grateful laughter. The morrow of all morrows would determine their ever, ever after.

The following day began with "good morning" as greeting words. A soft rain and bright sun accompanied the chirping of songbirds. The successful scholars strode forth with a confident air. It was a pleasant sight and sound to every eye and ear. Zhong Kui and his fellow successful candidates arrived at the palace gate. They were then ushered in and put into place. With bodies kowtowed against the ground, they dared not make a single sound. The emperor entered the room and took his seat upon the dragon's throne. All stayed motionless, as if made of stone.

23

The scholars received their rewards of office with heads bowed. All was well, at least for now. But when Zhong Kui went to receive his official first place commission, he made a mistake that would cost him his position. Out of curiosity, he raised his head to peek at the Son of Heaven, and by doing so, no office to him would be given. His eyes met directly with the emperor's gaze; Zhong Kui stared into the sun's very blaze. From the emperor came a gasp of shock, for what he saw made his pulse stop. The emperor quickly decided that this frightful demon-like man was something that should be driven off with a pounding of his hand. The emperor called for his guards to seize and remove Zhong Kui. The emperor ordered with a shout, "Take, take, take this beast out and away!"

The palace guards dragged Zhong Kui out and threw him headfirst down the palace steps. He landed at the bottom with a thud upon his chest. Blood issued forth, with a couple of teeth. He lay motionless, in stunned disbelief. His anger and sorrow built into a brewing storm, but what happened to him had been forewarned. He was the dragon who left home seeking a prize. But what he sought with all due effort was not realized. It was his offense to the monks and Buddha that brought an ill-conceived demon conspiracy that changed his figure and face. Now to the world and to himself, he was disgraced. For the things we do along the journey often have consequences at the end. Thus be careful of what you do and whom you do offend.

Zhong Kui howled to heaven, "What will become of me now?" Then, acting rashly, he dashed his head mightily against the palace gate, and with this sudden, brutish end, fulfilled his fate.

24

Chapter Three

Happy Willow
Boy, Scholar

Happy, sad, light, dark,
Sun, moon, silence, bark.
Opposing opposites everywhere,
Pulling, pushing, smiles, tears.
All is as meant to be,
Good or evil choices are for thee.

A young boy of only twelve,
In the heart of China do I dwell.
By Happy Willow am I known,
I thirst for knowledge like a parched stone.
Living, learning are you and I;
I, too, seek to thrive.

Parallel lives are often true,
A well-worn path is nothing new.
The past and present have many souls,
What should we value or reject—do you know?

25

The answers may not be found before you die,
Not everyone gets it right on their first try.
Even the leaf returns in spring,
Enjoy my story and see what it brings.

The camel's bellow broke the silence of my nap as I adjusted myself upon the sack of tea leaves. City life entered my eyes and ears. Brown-yellow dust veiled the sight of my mother as she called, "Happy Willow! Happy Willow!" My father was a butcher of meat, while my mother tended to our home. I was the only son, brother to none. My home was the city of Luoyang, Henan Province, China. This Yellow River Basin area is known as the "Cradle of Chinese Civilization." The Silk Road passes through our city as the main artery of China's commercial heart, and Luoyang has been the capital of China several times.

I was twelve years old. My distinguishing features were my long earlobes, slouching shoulders, and slight frame. My mother gave me the nickname Happy Willow. I had the physical frame of a young willow tree and the shy contentment of happiness. I was born in the year AD 1368, under the Ming dynasty's founding ruler, Emperor Hongwu. The Yuan dynasty, which had begun in AD 1279 under Emperor Kublai Khan, had succumbed to the decline that is the fate of all dynastic cycles. Emperor Hongwu, born a common peasant, had risen to become the Son of Heaven. His military campaigns as leader of the Red Turban Army and his nationalistic message of expelling the foreign Mongols were successful. Once free of the Mongol yoke, the emphasis was on reclaiming the Chinese culture—hence the saying, "Learn from the Tang and Song [dynasties]" of China's past.

My education came to me by way of a Taoist hermit known as Gnarled Pine, whom I met by chance and circumstance. Because I loved nature, I often hiked in the mountains outside the city. One day as I hiked, I came across a tiger sleeping in a grove of pines. I was closer than felt comfortable, so I tried to tiptoe away before the tiger noticed me. As I

26

turned, I stepped on a dry pine twig, and the sound of its snapping was like a firecracker going off. Startled, the tiger leapt to his feet, and I ran for my life, moving as swiftly as a hare, because I was fearful of becoming his lunch. Although I heard no growl from the animal and could not detect his pursuit, I didn't stop or look back until I reached a road populated by people traveling here and there. As I bent over to catch my breath, I heard a voice say, "Why do you inhale and exhale with such greed? God puts no limit on the air we breathe."

I looked up to see a man of craggy looks and crooked stance. He appeared to be middle-aged, as his hair and beard lacked the white snow of old age. He balanced himself with a walking staff, and he wore a white robe with a light blue sash. On his feet were the well-worn shoes of a traveler. He was Gnarled Pine.

We spoke until the hour grew late and the moon became known to us. I was intrigued and entranced by his manner of speech, as he spoke mostly in rhyme. I asked him if he would instruct me in the ways of reading and writing, and he agreed. This is how a butcher's son started on the path toward becoming a scholar and perhaps eventually a government official. As Gnarled Pine's pupil, I would become acquainted with the elementary skills of reading, writing, and thinking. Other aspects of my culture were fed into my being simply through living.

Chapter Four

Happy Willow
Boy, Scholar

The next morning, before my father left for work, and before I was awakened, Gnarled Pine spoke to my parents about tutoring me in reading and writing. This was a pleasant surprise to my parents, and they agreed to the lessons, as long as I completed my chores as usual. My family lacked the funds to pay for a formal education but had always wished that I could acquire learning to better myself in society. They saw Gnarled Pine's offer as a gift not to be declined.

Each morning after breakfast and chores, I would climb the mountain trail. It was a healthy hike to Gnarled Pine's thatched hut near the top of the mountain; it stood in a clearing of pine trees and wild chrysanthemums. The exercise nourished my lungs and awoke my body and mind. It was the autumn of AD 1368.

Inside Gnarled Pine's thatched hut were two rooms: one was his sleeping quarters, while the other contained a table, two chairs, writing materials, and many scrolls. Gnarled Pine drilled me daily in the art of calligraphy and the meaning of characters. He would say,

One climbs the mountain of knowledge step by step,
But the top itself can never be reached, so don't fret.
It's the climb itself that fills and strengthens our brain,
The summit itself is reached only by the vain.

Thereby, I learned that the scholar should be humble in his knowledge and that the learning itself is never ending. And so went by year one of my journey up the mountain.

In year two, Gnarled Pine introduced me to poems and stories that I was to memorize and recite on command. I learned the sayings and teachings of Confucius, Mencius, Lao Tzu, Buddha, and Damo. They were little-known men to me at the time, but Gnarled Pine's explanations of their teachings gave me an appreciation of their knowledge. When I questioned him, to understand more clearly the sometimes confusing meaning of the masters, he said,

Memorization will suffice for now,
Chew slowly, my young, hungry cow.
Understanding will come in due time,
For now, you are at the beginning of your climb.

Only later did I appreciate that the tenets of a philosophy are not always understood when first taught, but that seasons pass before clarity is found through experience and thought. Now, you see, even Gnarled Pine's rhyming was rubbing off on me; surely I was a pupil of this man named after a tree.

In year three, I was a tethered pony that needed to roam, and Gnarled Pine sensed it. He broadened my teachings to include composing poems and paintings. He instructed me to paint a scene for each poem I studied or wrote myself. Gnarled Pine even carved me a seal in the shape of a young willow tree with which I could sign my paintings. I treasured this seal, and I noticed that Gnarled Pine had a pine tree seal that he used to sign his paintings. He also had a tiger and a turtle seal, but I never saw him use them, so I asked him about them. He explained that those seals were carved and given to him by his Taoist master, Quiet Buffalo. He said that he used those seals to send messages to heaven.

"How so?" I asked.

Gnarled Pine replied that he would write a prayer request on a piece of paper, affix either the tiger or the turtle seal to it, and then burn the paper. The smoke would carry the message to heaven above.

"Then what?" I inquired.

Gnarled Pine only laughed and said that was for him to know and not me. As I knew the Taoist dabbled in magical arts, I accepted his explanation as an eccentric practice and left it at that.

One day in the winter of AD 1371, Gnarled Pine told me that his master, Quiet Buffalo, had taught him the following lesson:

We have two kinds of sight: the eyes with which we see the world itself,
And the mind's eye, with which we see things thought and felt.
While the first is a practical sense,
The second has more power and must be wisely spent.
Do not stray from what you know to what you feel,

31

For rash emotion is a senseless deal.
Whether a good man acts bad or a bad man acts good,
Heaven judges blindly, as it should.

A chill ran down my spine at Gnarled Pine's subtle warning and stern expression. Then a winter draft blew under the cabin door, and I blamed it for my chill. Only later would I learn how apt Gnarled Pine's words were.

Toward the end of the next summer, Gnarled Pine made a comment to me as he gazed at the horizon: "Soon the fish will travel downriver to the Ocean of Knowledge." He had no rhyme this time, and of this I took note. I sensed that our lessons were coming to a close. The next day would confirm my suspicion.

I dutifully climbed the mountain, as I had done for the past three years, but when I reached the cabin, I could not find Gnarled Pine. I waited until midafternoon for him to arrive, yet he did not appear. Suddenly, through the pine grove, I heard a growl and the rushing, crushing sound of an approaching beast. Instinctively I leapt to my feet and began to run, and when I turned to look back, I saw a tiger standing outside Gnarled Pine's hut. He let out a heart-chilling roar, and just as I had three years earlier, I ran for my life. When Gnarled Pine did not appear, I feared that he may have been eaten by the tiger. I ran home to alert my parents of my concern, and they relayed the following to me.

My mother said that in the morning after I had left to go visit Gnarled Pine, he visited my parents at our house. He told them that I had outgrown his teaching and that I needed some formal training. He knew of a school that would accept me as a pupil, as a favor to him. There would be no fee, only the debt of gratitude. As my mother spoke, happiness shined from her face, and tears perched on the rims of her eyelids.

Then my father spoke. "Son, since the time you were born, we have always wanted what is best for you. Gnarled Pine has offered such a path.

Beginning this autumn, you will travel downriver to attend the Yellow River Temple Academy and be trained by a scholar who, like you, was once a pupil of Gnarled Pine. Your trip will take three days by boat, but you will never be a moment from our hearts and minds. Do as your teacher instructs and make us proud. I am but a butcher of meat, but I can detect the best cuts, and so can Gnarled Pine. If he has set you on this course, then fate is at work."

These were perhaps the most words I had ever heard my father speak at one time. He was a sincere, quiet man, whose harsh looks belied his soft heart. I went to bed that night with hope and happiness, but it was mixed with despair and worry about what had happened to Gnarled Pine.

I waited one week before building up the courage to go back up the mountain to Gnarled Pine's hut. I saw no sign of him—or the tiger, thank god—but in my heart I hoped that Gnarled Pine was safe. A mountain hermit is one who wanders, and perhaps he would wander back into my life in the future. At least that was my hope.

Chapter Five

Happy Willow
Boy, Scholar

Scholar of merit, once pupil of Pine,
Voice of White Lotus who seeks the divine.
Teacher of teachers, humble and meek,
By strength of character, he supports the weak.

On behalf of the Pine he mentors the Willow,
With a soft approach, like a head on a pillow.
With each passing season the sapling grows,
In cloistered cultivation reached by a watery road.

The Yellow River Temple is his home,
He is still in one place, but his mind doth roam.
Through books, essays, poems, and ink,
He deciphers meaning and makes one think.

He is Gentle Cloud, loftier than all,
Livingly contently from autumn to fall.
Look up, and you see him above.
Gently dispensed lessons—his form of love.

The Yellow River Temple Academy was a select institution for young men who were chosen for their innate gifts or for the gifts given on their behalf. If not by nature, then by funds; either way, that was how things were done.

On a warm, drizzling September morning, I said good-bye to my parents on the riverbank's edge and proceeded downriver by boat. Two days passed of slow, meandering drift. These would be the last moments of drift in my life, for a regimen of academic study would be my path for the next six years.

On the morning of the third day, I surveyed my surroundings. Towering green-brown cliffs funneled the yellow-brown river water toward the horizon. I spotted roof tiles and locked my eyes on the emerging temple. It was in a remote location of surrounding wilds and life-giving springs. A crane flew overhead and pierced the air with a screeching cry as if announcing my arrival. The appeal of this place to the monks, who had built the isolated temple more than three hundred years ago, was apparent. It was seclusion they sought and seclusion they got. As the boat docked, a gentleman greeted me and introduced himself as Gentle Cloud. In me, Gentle Cloud said, he saw a younger version of himself, as he himself had once been a pupil of Gnarled Pine. Gentle Cloud had agreed to look after me and instruct me in the arts of a scholar. And so a new connection was forged, and the chain of brotherhood, bound by duty and honor, grew by one link more.

鶴山

Yellow River Temple Academy

It was Gentle Cloud who would mold me into a scholar and help me prepare for the civil service exams that would eventually launch my career as a government official. Gentle Cloud himself had been unable to take the exams in his youth—at the time, the Mongols of the Yuan dynasty had abandoned the practice. With the emergence of the Ming dynasty, Emperor Hongwu restored the examination system. But by that time Gentle Cloud's ambition had been cooled by age, and he found solace and satisfaction as a teacher. He hoped to pass his knowledge on to me to help me succeed in the exams and further my own happiness, for the glory of the Ming dynasty.

In his youth, Gentle Cloud became a member of the White Lotus Society, and he is a member to this day. The Society promotes the view that a messianic Buddha will come to unite the world. Its intentions are religious in nature—to help women and the poor—but it is also a subversive political organization with the goal of expelling the Mongols from China. During its reign, the Yuan dynasty banned the organization, and thereby it became a secret society. Eventually, one of its members, Hongwu, rose to military power, expelled the Mongol foreigners, and established the Ming dynasty. Gentle Cloud has never raised a sword, but his calligraphy brush has been an instrumental tool in spreading the message of the White Lotus Society.

Gentle Cloud, as I found out, was the teachers of all teachers. He opened up to me the vast ocean of knowledge of which Gnarled Pine had spoken. Through my studies of the Confucian classics, Taoism, and Buddhism, three treasures became known to me. I found that all three are compatible, and none need exclude the others. Confucianism speaks of the proper relationship of people, society, and government. Taoism speaks to the natural way of life, as exhibited in nature, and how it applies to living one's life. Life does not need to be examined but simply experienced. Finally, Buddhism is, fundamentally, a moral code by which humans should live and die, over and over again until

38

Enlightenment; when one realizes one's own Buddha nature and practice forthwith. The cycle of birth and death is then extinguished and nirvana is reached.

Toward the end of my sixth year, Gentle Cloud said I was ready to begin my march toward the high goal: the imperial exam. I had already passed all of the required local and provincial exams, and now my ultimate goal was finally before me. I would take the imperial exam in the capital city. The imperial exam itself was more complex than the lower exams. The essay questions needed to be answered in a format known as the eight-legged essay, which was highly structuralized and complex. Therefore, knowledge of the Confucian classics and a persuasive argument alone were not enough to pass the exam; the structure of the essay was of equal importance.

Gentle Cloud drilled me in the eight-legged essay format during my six years of formal training and for two subsequent years of practice for the imperial exam. Now, on the verge of taking the imperial exam—nicknamed the "spider exam"—I felt ready to tackle it.

The last lesson Gentle Cloud gave to me was by way of a poem on the virtue and vice of being a government official:

Creature of eight legs,
By spinning a web, you don't need to beg.
Winged or crawling insects enter your domain,
With evenhandedness, make your name.
Eat, drink, stay thin, and don't grow fat,
Watch out for hands that would crush you flat.
By gift of craft or crafty gifts, a spider climbs.
Ascending up or down is due to the times.
So sit and rest when needed upon a shelf,
For what you do, to you also shall be dealt.

The following is the message the poem conveyed:

Creature of eight legs,
(This is the eight-legged essay you need to pass to become an official.)
By spinning a web, you don't need to beg.
(By writing a skilled essay, you will earn rewards.)
Winged or crawling insects enter your domain,
(People of status and commoners will be under your authority.)
With evenhandedness, make your name.
(Be just to all, and you will earn a good reputation.)
Eat, drink, stay thin, and don't grow fat.
(Use power thriftily and avoid excessive power.)
Watch out for hands that would crush you flat.
(Be careful of adversaries.)
By gift of craft or crafty gifts, a spider climbs.
(An official may rise due to good work or due to bribes.)
Ascending up or down is due to the times.
(An official's position is precarious due to random changes.)
So sit and rest when needed upon a shelf,
(Be content with what you have, as dictated by situations.)
For what you do, to you also shall be dealt.
(How you treat others will result in how they treat you.)

One night a month prior to the imperial exam, I gazed upward and noticed two falling stars in the western sky—a large star trailed by a smaller one. Now, a falling star may be an ill omen. That I had been gazing at the sky at that exact moment made me wonder if it was a sign meant for me. The next morning, word came by boat that my father had fallen ill and was on the brink of death. I quickly set out for home.

Upon reaching Luoyang, I stopped at the White Horse Temple, the first Buddhist temple in China. There I bought incense from an old woman, lit the incense, and placed it into the sand of a burner. I said a prayer for my father and hoped the incense smoke would carry my message asking for the compassion of Buddha to heal my father.

40

Upon returning home, I found my father barely able to speak. Mother attended to him with soup and tea, but he found it hard to swallow. Mother said the doctors had given him little hope of survival. My father motioned to me to come near. I put my ear near his mouth, and he whispered, "Soon I will die. Pass the imperial exam and look after your mother." No words breached his lips after that moment. The next day I said my good-byes and left on my mission to get to the capital, pass the exam, and fulfill my father's dying request. The exam would not only determine my future but my mother's as well. I was now in the latter half of my twenty-fourth year.

Chapter Six

Happy Willow
Boy, Scholar

Upon reaching the capital of Nanjing, I found a local inn and settled in for the night. The imperial exam would take place at the palace in two days. On the evening of the next day, as I was eating supper, a man with a familiar face walked into the inn. He was an old childhood friend. As we spotted each other, tears streamed down his face, and I knew that my father had passed away. Protocol dictated that I return home immediately for my father's funeral and to begin a three-year mourning period. Such was the way to show respect for one's parent. But my practical and ambitious side knew I needed to take the imperial exam on behalf of my mother and myself. Now I was the head of the family; I was pulled between honoring my father and doing my duty toward my mother. I chose duty.

I did not sleep that night as I debated my decision over and over again. As morning broke, however, my mind was set, and I headed off to the palace for the exam. Once inside, I settled in for the exam, and when it began, my tiredness and the weight of worry fell aside as I focused intently on the task at hand. My calligraphy brush flourished as if guided by Gentle Cloud and the ancient masters. Poetically I crafted an eight-legged essay. As I paused to apply more ink to my brush and gather my thoughts, I sighed and peered up at a beam high above me. To my surprise, there sat an owl staring back at me. Our eyes met but for a moment; then off he flew, silently, out a window. The owl in Chinese culture is an ill omen, as it carries souls to the afterworld. It was very strange to see one during daylight because they are creatures of the night. From that moment forward, I felt chilled and unfocused, but luckily the exam was coming to a close. I finished the last few lines of my essay the best I could and greeted the friendly embrace of relief that followed.

Behind the scenes at the palace, a treacherous scheme was underway. Some eunuch servants of the emperor had been bribed by a powerful and wealthy minister to ensure that his son would place first in the imperial exam. Included in the conspiracy was an unscrupulous palace scholar who took action to fix the results. He had to do so without arousing the suspicion of the other officials, and herein was the challenge. But as he had oversight of the exam grading process, he had full access to the exams.

The grading was completed by numerous scholars, and unknown to me at the time, I had placed first in the exam. Thus it was my exam the scheming scholar had to invalidate in order to put the minister's son's exam in first place. The wayward scholar went into action. He called to examine for himself both my first-place exam and the minister's son's exam. All of the exams were copied over in red ink in order to obscure the original author. Behind closed doors he recopied my essay in red ink again; he was adept at counterfeiting. In doing so he subtly changed a few characters that upon closer examination appeared to be cryptic metaphors that slandered the emperor and challenged his authority. Such an insult was unacceptable, and nothing good would come of it. To seal the deal, he bullied and bribed the other palace scholars into ranking the minister's son's essay in first place, as a consensus was needed to do so. It was a bold and dangerous move by the scholar, but money motivates some men more than does morals.

When I arrived at the palace the next day to learn the official exam results, I was arrested and thrown into prison. I was shocked by the turn of events, and horrified to learn of the charges against me. I was beaten and starved for three days, as guards sought to extract a false confession regarding what I had written in my essay. After this method bore no fruit, the group of conspiring eunuchs, the scholar, and the minister sought to get rid of me as fast as possible for fear of having their scheme exposed by a more thorough investigation.

On the morning of the fourth day, my will was weak and my body sapped of strength. I saw no way out of my situation. A great sense of hopelessness filled my whole being as the conspiracy continued to grow. The palace prison guard watching me had been bought off. He told me if I confessed I would be sentenced to ten years' hard labor at a prison camp on Hainan Island off the southern coast of China. If I didn't confess, I would be executed by beheading. Such was the psychological pressure put on me in order to extract a false confession.

What I did not know was that a more thorough investigation had been started once the emperor heard that I was a pupil of Gentle Cloud. He knew the good reputation of my teacher, and this cast doubts in his mind that a student of Gentle Cloud would insult the emperor. The emperor ordered a separate secret investigation by his spies to see if there was more to this situation than met the eye.

On the fifth day, a new plan was set into motion: to dispatch me and end the swirling controversy surrounding my arrest. That morning, the prison guard gave me a gourd of water for my thirst, which I eagerly accepted. But as I raised the gourd to my lips, I caught the guard watching, seemingly waiting for me to drink. I made a split-second decision to close my lips tight against the mouth of the gourd. I only pretended to drink, for at that moment I suspected—correctly—that the water had been poisoned. I then lay down with my back to the guard, moaned a few times for effect, and pretended to succumb to the poison.

45

The guard walked away, and I felt a sense of relief but also a strong sleepiness. The poison was so potent that even the minuscule amount that passed my lips had had an effect. I drifted off into a black silence not knowing if I would live. In that moment, I thought of my parents, resigned myself to whatever fate had in store, and sought to escape the only way I could—through death.

Chapter Seven

Zhong Kui

"Welcome to hell, Happy Willow. I, too, did not fare well on the imperial exam. So now we both live here in the home of the damned. I have an army, thousands strong—condemned souls of deeds done wrong. Only lotus souls grow in the fields of heaven, while others must earn what to the righteous is given. I am the head demon queller, Zhong Kui. I serve the emperor by night and by day.

"It has been a long time since Emperor Gaozu threw me out of his palace and did me wrong. But the emperor felt regret for his act when he heard I was gone. He honored me with an official title and burial, with the help of Du Ping. I was touched by this honor, and this pledge I did sing:

I know now it was devilish demons that changed my figure and face,
I suspected the monks, but this was a mistake.
I vow to rid the world of demons and ghosts;
This is my promise and no drunken boast.
While my suicide sin has not served me well,
I'll redeem myself by serving from hell.

47

I fear no demon, ghost, or man;
Ridding the world of evil is my plan.
As long as I'm dead and dwell among spirits,
Demons and ghosts hear my oath and learn to fear it.

"Since this oath I have served in the shadows and out of sight. But to the Tang emperor Ming Huang I made myself known one night. The emperor was ill and fell asleep. During this time, a small demon did creep. The emperor dreamt that the demon was stealing his goods. I entered his dream and did what I could. I grabbed the small demon and gouged out his eyes. Then I gobbled him up, to the emperor's surprise. The emperor said, 'Who are you that came to my aid?' I replied, 'I'm the demon queller, known as Zhong Kui.'

"The emperor then awoke from his dream and to his guards shouted and screamed, 'Go get the court painter Wu Daozi. I have an image that needs recording for all to see.' The emperor's sickness had gone away, but the dream he had had would not fade. Wu Daozi listened to the emperor's description, and the painting that resulted was a remarkable depiction. The emperor was astonished by the artist's painting. He said, 'You must have had the same dream as I. How else could this image you surmise?'

"Wu Daozi replied, 'I know of the story of Zhong Kui. I heard of his legend in days gone by. Now with your words mixed with my paint and from what I have known, I created this image not by myself alone.'

"The emperor was pleased with the words of Wu Daozi. He issued an edict to have the painting copied and distributed throughout the empire for all to see. The edict read:

Hang this image at all city gates;
Let it be known that demons do tempt their fate.
For from evil, Zhong Kui guards all men,
From demons and ghosts he will defend.

48

For what service he could not do in life,
He serves the emperor by day and night.
He turned misfortune into a good deed,
So rest, fellow citizens, he works for thee.

"So, Happy Willow, will you join me now and serve as one of my men? One can find redemption in service to my ends. But as for me, I've chosen my duty here forever. I can think of no service that suits me better. Here, let me give you some wine while you make your decision. This nectar of grain will refresh your wisdom…"

Happy Willow
Boy, Scholar

Zhong Kui tossed the cup of wine into my face, and gasping for air, I did awake! I said to myself it was but a dream or nightmare and not what it seemed. In fact, imperial guards had thrown a bucket of water on me to see if I was still alive. The treacherous scheme had been exposed, and thankfully, the poison was not enough for me to die. Just then, I noticed two red bats fly past the window of my prison cell. Curious, I stood on a stool and looked out. I saw a man with a sword and red cape running away into the moonlit dark. The man turned back, and showed his frightful face. "It is he! It's Zhong Kui!" I yelled. "The man from my dream who serves from hell." But he was gone by the time I'd spoken the words. Concealed by the night, he slipped into the mist and out of sight.

Chapter Eight

Happy Willow
Boy, Scholar

I was escorted out of the prison, through the courtyard, and into the palace hall. Palace academy officials were lined up to the left and right. At the far end of the room sat the emperor. The air was humid and sweat poured from my brow. I was brought before the emperor, and I assumed a kowtow position. The emperor ordered me to rise, and I stood, weak-kneed, before the Son of Heaven.

From behind I heard the clinking and dragging of chains. I peered back and saw a group of men linked together in bondage. Their heads hung in shame, and bruises of blue, black, and purple marked their faces. One man was the scholar and another was the prison guard who had given me the poison; the rest were eunuchs, whose shaved heads and feminine demeanor gave away their identity.

An officer of justice then rose to begin the proceedings. He explained that one of the eunuchs had confessed to the scheme. The interrogators had told the eunuch that a quick confession would spare him the torture and death penalty that awaited him. A man who lacks integrity initially would lack the integrity needed to conceal a scheme when threatened by punishment. The ship of conspiracy had sprung a leak, and this eunuch was the first rat to abandon ship. The other offenders had been rounded up and tortured to extract their confessions. The wealthy and powerful minister who had funded the evil plot drank poison as soldiers pounded on the door of his home. It was the same type of poison that had been given to me.

The justice official ended his presentation, and the emperor rose to speak. He declared that the offenders would be executed immediately, except for the eunuch had who confessed first. He would have his tongue cut out, his ears and nose clipped off, and a criminal mark branded on his face. He was then exiled to the prison camp on Hainan Island. The guilty were ushered out of the great hall, and I stood before the emperor.

The emperor apologized for the misunderstanding and ordered that I be given an official position of my choosing. My relief was immediate, and I thanked the emperor. I yearned to return home to Luoyang so that I could honor my father and care for my dear mother. Therefore I requested a post in Luoyang, and so it was granted. My heart belonged to the mountains of Henan, the city of Luoyang, and the home of my family.

The sweet smell of peonies buffered Luoyang as I approached the outskirts of the city. It was springtime, and I was experiencing a rebirth of my own. I knew the location of my father's grave from the friend who had brought the news of my father's death. It was there that I headed immediately upon reaching the city. When in the capital of Nanjing, I had chosen duty over honor for the benefit of my mother and me. Now, on my return, my first obligation was to honor my father by visiting his grave.

I thought of the many memories that were embedded in my heart and mind. My thoughts raced with the cadence of my steps. Each step brought me closer to my father and each thought closer to his spirit. My mind rambled with poetic stylings...

As strong as an oak, he sired a son,
As weak as a willow, I was the one.
He cared for me from my day of birth,
I hung onto him, my anchor on this earth.
I was his opposite in many ways,
But he never discouraged the interests I craved.
Now he is gone,
And I long.

I long for his proud glance,
That I caught, here and there, by chance.
I long for his pat on my back,
His gruff but loving tact.
He was a man to admire,
To emulate him, I aspire.
Now he is gone,
And I long.

I reached his grave, knelt down, and placed my hand on the naked earth mound. A breeze cooled my face and dried my tears. It was a breath of nature's grace. I knew this day would come someday, but one pushes aside such unwanted thoughts. To embrace such contemplation seems a traitor's lot. When cricket chirps marked the end of day, I left for home.

In accordance with custom, I was permitted to delay taking office to observe the three-year mourning period. I was given a small government pension, and a position would be awaiting me once the mourning period was over. I lived the life of an idle scholar. My hair grew long and my long, thin beard could have rivaled that of the Han dynasty general Guan Yu. During the Three Kingdom era, following the fall of the Han dynasty, Guan Yu's severed head was buried in Luoyang by his admiring enemy, Cao Cao. Luckily, I still had my head.

I spent my days looking after Mother, reading, writing, and painting. Also, I often hiked up into the mountains and strolled in the countryside. My face became familiar to the local peasants, as theirs did to me. We would often have conversations as I came and went. I made friends with one farmer whom the locals called Nine Fingers. As a young boy, his right thumb had been severed by a garden hoe during horseplay with friends. Nine Fingers was an uncommon commoner, in that he was literate and fancied calligraphy. As his right hand had only four fingers, he trained himself to master the brush with his left hand. He often sold his calligraphy compositions in the city market alongside his crops. Many of his works copied the poems of Du Fu, a son of Henan, and one of China's most famous poets.

Nine Fingers had a daughter named Fruit Fruit, who was eighteen years old. Her parents named her Fruit Fruit because she was the fruit of their fruitful union. Nine Fingers taught her how to read and write, and she had a gift in the poetic arts. Her body was thin and straight like a bamboo stalk, while her face was melon shaped with prominent cheeks. Her skin was plum-blossom white, while most peasants had the yellowish burnt-tan skin of countryside dwellers. Some said this marked her as destined for city life and marriage to a nobleman. As I would find out, Nine Fingers had me in mind as his son-in-law.

Nine Fingers had sent a matchmaker to speak with my mother, and she, in turn, spoke with me. Mother encouraged me to pluck this rare fruit before other suitors became aware of her. I knew Fruit Fruit because of my relationship with Nine Fingers, and I needed little encouragement, as my desires already coincided with their wishes. Fruit Fruit's eyes and smile expressed a true heart, intelligence, and a playful kindness. Some might say that she was blessed in marrying a young scholar with a future as a government official, but I knew that, truly, I was the fortunate one.

54

We wed on the sixth day of the ninth moon, an auspicious day picked by Nine Fingers. Fruit Fruit moved into our home. The three-year mourning period was coming to a close, and my career as an official was about to begin.

Chapter Nine

Stephen
Author & Artist

During the sixth century AD there ruled a wicked governor of Henan Province. He dealt in all manner of treachery and debauchery. Power and pleasure were his vices. Now, we all have a tale written of not so good deeds for god to read. But how does a rotten fruit become fresh again? How does a bad man change within? Or, in the mind of the governor, how does one avoid judgment and punishment for one's sins? This was the thought that beset the governor's conscience as his hours in life grew late. A never-ending life he sought, to escape his fate.

Night after night, the governor's brain churned. He slept little, with much angst of mind. He searched frantically for a way to forever extend his life. Murder by conspiracy, blackmail, theft, and adultery had been his trade. No wonder then that he feared what existed beyond the grave. Like a worm boring into a peach, his conscience drilled into his mind in search for peace. He thought, what have I gained but material stuff and deep regret due to ill-gotten gains? What will be my existence when this life no longer remains? What lies beyond, which frightens me so? What punishment awaits me when my pulse grows cold? I must hold off judgment by avoiding death. Life never-ending shall be my quest.

The governor sought out potions, magical peaches, and charlatans with spells of immortality. Nothing seemed to work, but he searched on and on to escape the grips of hell.

Then one day the governor's advisor told him of a Buddhist monk who traveled across the Yangtze River upon a single reed, then rebuked the emperor and took his leave. "Perhaps this holy man has the answer you seek," the advisor said. "He now sits in a cave near the Shaolin Temple staring at a wall, in deep meditation to Buddha's call. Bodhidharma was his Indian name, but Damo was the Chinese name by which he was known. Once a prince from India, who sought enlightenment instead of a throne, he came to China to spread Zen Buddhism, but who could understand his wisdom?"

The governor grew excited by this news, so off he went to find this man who came from a foreign land.

The governor arrived at the Shaolin Temple and asked for Damo. A monk said that Damo usually meditated in a cave on the hillside above the temple. "But you will not find him there now," said the monk.

"Where has he gone?" the governor eagerly inquired. The monk replied that Damo was meditating at the lotus pond, down a beaten path. Off went the governor hoping to find his answer.

The governor came to a large lotus pond that stretched out before him. Kingfishers darted into the water seeking tiny fish, cranes stalked about looking for frogs, while turtles sunbathed on logs. The governor searched about but saw no man. He spied a young boy riding on the back of a water buffalo and spoke to him: "Have you seen an Indian monk by the name of Damo?"

The boy giggled and pointed to the middle of the pond. The pond was thick with lotus leaves that obscured the view, but he was able to make out the monk, who appeared to be sitting on top of the water.

The governor yelled for Damo to come ashore, but there was no answer. This perturbed the governor, but he did not want to offend the monk, so he waded in and made his way to Damo. Mud and muck squished between his toes. Green-blue leaves and white lotus flowers brushed against him. The pond was deeper than it looked, and he soon became submerged up to his chest. As he moved closer, he noticed that Damo was sitting just above the water on a level meditation rock. The governor stopped in front of Damo. Never before at a loss for words, the governor now stood silent. He felt a presence in Damo that left him frozen in mind and body. The governor waited for Damo to acknowledge him.

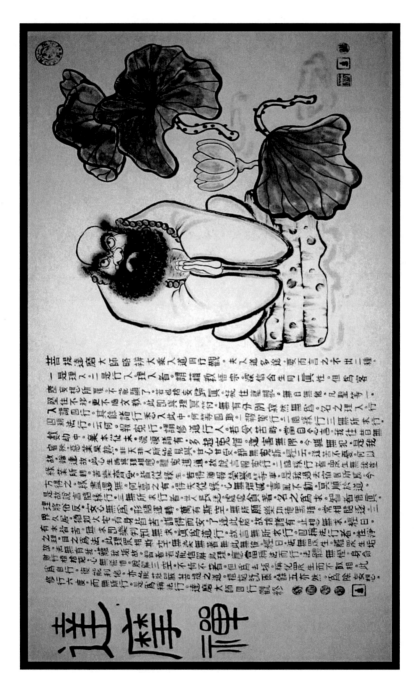

達摩

Damo meditating at lotus pond

60

Damo had the dark complexion of a monk from southern India. His bushy beard was black, and a half moon-ring of hair surrounded his baldhead. He was tough and gruff, but also kind and compassionate. Such was this saintly sage.

Damo sat with his eyes shut and his expression grim. He then opened his eyes, looked intensely at the governor, and spoke. "I've heard of you, as you have of me, so I know what you seek with such greed. You search for an answer out of fright, to avoid your oncoming plight. Karma is heavy on your mind. Better to live forever, you think, than to answer for your crimes."

The governor's head dropped in shame, and he thought, What Damo says is true. He sees the black stain of bad karma on my heart and mind. Pray, I do, that he gives me a chance to atone for these sins and crimes.

Damo began to speak again after a long pause of focused meditation, as if he were communicating with someone in his mind. "If it were up to me I would send you away to face karma's justice in hell, but the Bodhisattva Guan Yin, goddess of mercy and compassion, whose compassion outweighs mine, persuaded me to put the burden of penance on you with a spell. If I tell you what you want to know, you will be transformed, the summer cicada reborn again. You will have long life only to right your sins. Immortality is out of the question, but you will face a better rebirth once you do pass from this earth.

"Through good deeds you shall guide others on a rightful path. Guan Yin will keep an eye on you so don't deceive. It was your conscience that brought you here today, and that same conscience guides your way. Now, come over here, and I'll whisper a message into your ear, and when the time is right, pass it along to break the spell. By then, you will fear no more death or hell. Good karma will supplant bad karma, and these karmic seeds shall put you on the right path in the next life."

61

Damo whispered his message into the governor's ear, and physical changes did appear. His spine became crooked and twisted like a pine; his face became craggy and aged like bark; his back grew bulges and gnarled knots. One could no longer recognize his former self, but to change inside he would have to do that himself.

Damo spoke one last time: "Your former self is lost to time. From now on you will be known as Gnarled Pine. Inside and out you are twisted by wrongful actions and regretful thoughts; never forget the message you got. Roam these mountains and the Taoist hermit Quiet Buffalo will find you one day. Though mute, he will teach you the way; but death shall greet you if you stray. He shall give you a gift to extend your life. Now be off and out of my sight."

Gnarled Pine picked up a fallen tree branch as a walking staff upon leaving the pond, and off he went to right his wrongs.

Damo crossing the Yangtze River on a reed

Damo meditating in cave

Chapter Ten

Stephen
Author & Artist

Gnarled Pine roamed the Song Mountains for thirty days, not knowing where to go so Quiet Buffalo would find him. He lived off the land, eating roots, berries, bugs, and plants. He had never had to fend for himself, and the experience was very humbling. This suffering was meant to break him of his selfish, earthly desires and to help him focus on inner transformation. He realized that desire without restraint was life without meaning. As governor, he could never sate his appetite for power, pleasure, and material wealth. The more he accumulated, the more he wanted. He had gorged himself but never felt filled.

One night as Gnarled Pine lay down to sleep, he heard the sounds of hoofbeats. He sat up and stared in the direction of the sound, ears set as keenly as a bat's. There, on the crest of the hill, an outline of a water buffalo appeared against the backdrop of a full moon. The buffalo stopped, grunted, and sniffed the cool air. Picking up the scent of Gnarled Pine, it headed in his direction. The buffalo came down the hill and disappeared into a shallow spot. When it crested the next rise, instead of a buffalo there walked a large man. Gnarled Pine scrambled to his feet in uncertainty. The man was a giant, easily six feet six, with broad shoulders and a bald head; a wispy beard hung from his chin. Judging by his girth, he must have weighed about four hundred pounds. Gnarled Pine shook with trepidation as the man approached, but once he saw the gentleness of the man's eyes, his thumping heart began to calm and he felt no danger. The man bowed slightly to acknowledge Gnarled Pine, who likewise bowed back; the introduction was complete without a word. He was Quiet Buffalo.

When morning broke, Quiet Buffalo gestured for Gnarled Pine to follow him, and they walked up into the mountains to Quiet Buffalo's cabin. It was so high up that one could touch low-hanging, dewy clouds, and the path there was so treacherous and rugged that few would be able to find the location—a perfect spot for a Taoist hermit.

When Gnarled Pine entered the cabin, he noticed two things. First, the home was full of scrolls—here, there, and everywhere. These were the writings and paintings of Quiet Buffalo. Because he was mute, he had even more need than most to communicate with written words and images. Second, the simple exterior of the home stood in sharp contrast to the ornately carved tables, chairs, and woodwork of the interior. Gnarled Pine had unknowingly learned his first two lessons: the simple exterior of a person can never match the complexity of the interior, and the power of simple observation is often more insightful than a lecture by tongue.

That was how Gnarled Pine spent his years: studying the writings of Quiet Buffalo and learning of the ancient masters, roaming the mountains and countryside of Henan Province, and doing good deeds. He toiled in soil to help peasants grow crops, he taught many children and old people how to read and write, and in the mountains he picked rare medicinal herbs for the sick. As a wandering teacher of morals, reading, and writing, he provided to others a more fulfilling life. But more important, he was a teacher to himself. He saw that in small, simple ways he had more power than a multitude of government officials. He realized that, one peck of rice at a time, he could eventually outweigh the bushels of evil karma that he had acquired. His long life was spent doing penance on earth.

One day while he was studying, Gnarled Pine asked Quiet Buffalo about his seal, a buffalo with a man riding on its back, which he used to sign his writings and paintings. Quiet Buffalo picked up his brush and began to write. "I am the buffalo that carried Lao Tzu into the desert when he left this earthly world. After years of loyal service, Lao Tzu used his magical Taoist powers and changed me into a man. Lao Tzu first carved this seal, and then he wrote a prayer on paper, affixed the seal, and burned the paper. Smoke rose to the heavens, and poof! I took the form of a man."

Gnarled Pine then asked how Quiet Buffalo was able to transform back into a buffalo. Quiet Buffalo wrote that since the seal was carved by the hand of Lao Tzu himself, it was the most powerful transformation seal known to man. But only he had the power to use it. In mortal hands it had no power; he, however, could use it to transform into any kind of mammal, bird, fish, or insect on earth.

Quiet Buffalo then removed the top of a drinking gourd sitting on his desk and tipped out the gift that Damo had spoken of. It was a longevity crane seal, carved by Lao Tzu many years ago to ensure longevity to whoever used it. Quiet Buffalo instructed Gnarled Pine to use the seal every 108 years to extend his life again and again until he had expunged his sins.

Quiet Buffalo then asked, in writing, if Gnarled Pine would like him to carve a transformation seal for him. Gnarled Pine's eyes grew wide with excitement, and he jumped at the offer by requesting a multitude of transformation seals. Quiet Buffalo looked down and walked away. Gnarled Pine realized that a simple yes would have sufficed as an answer of gratitude. His display of greedy zeal had disappointed Quiet Buffalo, and Gnarled Pine apologized for the offense. Quiet Buffalo accepted the apology, sat down, and carved two seals for Gnarled Pine.

The first was a turtle seal. The turtle is gentle, slow to act, and well protected. The seal would be useful when Gnarled Pine needed to protect himself against beasts in the wild mountains or to hide from people. The second was a tiger seal. The tiger is powerful and mighty and is king of beasts in China. The seal would be used when force was required to survive. The two creatures were yin and yang symbols of the animal world.

Quiet Buffalo wrote, "Use the turtle seal when you need to be passive in behavior, and use the tiger seal when you need to be aggressive." He then handed the seals to Gnarled Pine, who treasured them the rest of his life.

Lao Tzu and Quiet Buffalo

Chapter Eleven

Quiet Buffalo
Taoist Master

I, Quiet Buffalo, was the water buffalo that day at the lotus pond when Damo gave his message to Gnarled Pine. I have been a longtime observer of men. I've seen battles and peace, peace and battles; such is the way of men. My master, Lao Tzu, was born in the sixth century BC. He brought to this world a philosophy: take action by doing nothing at all. Nature shows us the path, so heed its call.

Lao Tzu said, "The bamboo bends with the wind, while the pine stands straight against the day." But when to be one and when to be the other is the decision that ultimately exemplifies your own wisdom. I'll relay to you an adventure of mine, long before I met Gnarled Pine.

I made my home in the Song Mountains of Henan Province. With my transformation seal, I would often roam. One day as the sun shone bright, I heard a faint crying, out of my sight. I saw black vultures circling a field. What had they spied for their meal? I went to investigate and found a baby girl abandoned and exposed to die, not uncommon in a land where boys were the prize. A famine that year had been sweeping the land, and this one more mouth to feed was not in the plan. I scooped up the girl into my arms, when from behind, a growl did indicate harm. A very hungry tiger stalked us from the high, dry grass. I had no time to use my transformation seal—I had to act fast. Though I was in the form of a man, I still had water buffalo strength in my body and hands. The tiger charged and we met in a grasp; body against body we wrested through the crackling grass. Fangs, fur, and claws pitted against my strength. I grabbed him around the neck, squeezed, and yanked. His limbs grew limp as I held on tight. I continued to choke with all my might. Then I saw the baby girl watching with tears in her eyes, and what happened next came as a complete surprise. She raised her right hand as if signaling, "Please cease." I paused and then let go of the unconscious beast. She crawled to the tiger and placed her tiny hand on his wet nose, and upon her touch the tiger arose. The tiger looked at her kind eyes and slight smile, purred softly, and walked away. The tiger, as I, sensed in her an uncommon compassion for all living beings. Buddha would be proud of what I had seen. I named her Guan Yin, meaning Observing the Cries of This World. I would take care of this precious baby girl.

I took baby Guan Yin home to my mountain cabin. Upon arrival I noticed her forehead was very warm. Having been exposed so long to the elements, she had acquired a high fever. Also, blue spots were breaking out on her skin. I had a book on medicinal cures given to me by Lao Tzu. Inside was a treasure trove of natural remedies, both botanical and zoological. I searched the book for the baby's symptoms and came across a sickness known as blue-spotted fever. This had to be the sickness, as it was the only one that caused blue spots. It was a rare ailment that needed an even rarer prescription. The recipe for the

71

potion read, "Obtain molted skin of tiger cicada, red snail slime, and the glandular secretions of hermit toad and lotus toad; mix with tea and drink." I would have to act quickly to acquire said ingredients, as the sickness would progress quickly from fever to paralyses to death. Without treatment, she would survive no more than two days. Alongside the ingredients, the recipe gave the geographical locations of the creatures from which I could obtain the four items. I wrapped baby Guan Yin in blankets and placed her on my bed, and off I went.

First, I searched for the lotus toad. This was the easiest to find of the four, as it could be found at any lotus pond. I used my transformation seal to change into an eagle. Taking this form would allow me to travel quickly and would give me the keen eyesight needed to spy a toad from above. I swooped down the mountain to the lotus pond near the Shaolin Temple and circled above. A lotus toad is brown with a white underbelly. While not a frog, it keeps close to lotus ponds to lay its eggs. After a circle or two, I spotted a fat specimen sunning on a rock. I dived down in stealthy silence and plucked the toad with careful skill so as not to harm it with my sharp talons. Back to the cabin I flew, where I put down the toad and changed back into a man. It took the transformation seal process for me to change into a certain creature, but I needed only the mind to release the form and change back into a man. I placed the toad in a box for safekeeping.

Next I searched for a hermit toad, a rare species of toad that lived in high mountains and hid in the tiny caves of rock outcrops. The toad was brown with multicolored spots and warts. It would be harder to find because of its shy nature. I used the transformation seal to change into a wild boar and off I went. With my powerful snout and tusks, I could easily forage about to locate the toad. I ran about sniffing, snuffing, and rooting in rocky locations. Like true hermits, these toads did not want to be found. After about an hour, I picked up a toad scent around a rocky formation. I changed back into a man and searched the crevasses and holes for a toad. I reached into a small crevasse with my hand and, sure enough, I felt a lumpy, bumpy toad holed up inside. I pulled it out, hiked back to my cabin, and placed it in a box for safekeeping.

Now I was off to find the molted skin of a tiger cicada. The tiger cicada had a two-year life cycle, at the end of which it would emerge from underground and shed its skin. The tiger cicada got its name from its black-and-orange striped markings. Luckily for Guan Yin, according to the timeline in the book of medicinal cures, this was a year that the tiger cicada would appear. I used the transformation seal and changed into an oriole. Off I flew, from one forest range to the next, searching for a tiger cicada brood, but I had no such luck before darkness fell. I holed up in a tree for the night.

That night I searched my mind for how I would be able to locate the tiger cicadas when day broke. Then, above me, I heard an owl hooting from a hollow in the tree. I flew to a branch near the hole and saw a mother owl and her chicks. I chirped to her my situation and inquired if she knew where any tiger cicadas were located. She hooted back that with her superior hearing she would search above the forest canopy for the singing sound of the cicadas. Her hearing was so acute that even from miles away she could even make out the species of cicada she heard singing. Off she flew and circled high in the sky. She returned in just a few moments and said that she'd located a brood far off to the south. As time was of the essence, and I could not locate them myself at night, I explained to her my predicament and asked for her help. As a mother she sympathized with my situation and agreed to retrieve the molted tiger cicada skin for me. I stayed and guarded the chicks. Before dawn she returned with the skin. I thanked her for her help and flew back to my cabin as daylight broke over the horizon.

Each time I returned to the cabin, I would check on baby Guan Yin. Her skin was sweat covered and her rigid limbs signaled the onset of paralysis. I had to act fast to find the last species, the red snail.

The red snail has a red body and blue shell. According to the medicine book, this species could be found in the yellow-bamboo grove on Song Mountain, not far from my cabin. While the location was close, the snail was extremely rare and would be particularly difficult to find. I ran to the location of the vast yellow-bamboo grove and had to think hard about how to locate the red snail in time to save the baby. I would need to use my transformation seal to become a predator of snails, for such a creature would have the instincts to locate its prey much faster than a human could. I used the seal to turn myself into a beetle. I could use my antennae to pick up the odor that emanates from the slime trail of a snail. I scurried across the forest floor and picked up the scent of a snail. I tracked it to a bamboo stalk. I proceeded up the stalk in a hurry, hoping to catch sight of the snail. In my eagerness I forged ahead too fast and found myself tangled in a spider web. I fought to free myself but spotted a spider moving in for the kill. I had to leave my beetle form and change back into a man to save my life. In an instant, I found myself sitting on the ground with a spider perched on my nose. It had been a very close call. I stood up and searched the bamboo stalk, and there toward the top, I spotted the red snail making its way upward. I bent the bamboo stalk down and plucked the snail off with ease. Then I hurried back home to assemble the medicinal potion.

Baby Guan Yin was holding on to dear life, but her breathing was becoming shallower. I grabbed a small ceramic bowl and placed the molted tiger cicada skin inside. I grabbed a toad with each hand and squeezed very gently; a milky secretion dripped from each of their backs into the bowl. Finally I wiped the snail's muscular foot around the bowl as slime oozed out. I then added some tea and mixed the concoction with a chopstick. I held baby Guan Yin in my arms and slowly poured the potion ever so gently into her mouth and down her throat. I placed her on my bed, and in exhaustion I drifted off to sleep.

The next morning I was awakened by the joyful laughter of baby Guan Yin. She sat on the bed playing with the toads and snail that helped save her life. I checked her condition and found that the blue spots were gone and her fever had broken. I sighed with great relief, and my reward was a soft smile and healthy happiness in her eyes. Later that day, out of gratitude, I returned the toads and snail from whence they came.

Guan Yin's legend would go on from there, as others have written. She had been discarded with no mercy or compassion, yet she herself became the symbol of mercy and compassion as the Bodhisattva Guan Yin.

Lotus toad

Hermit toad

78

Tiger cicadas

Red snail

Chapter Twelve

Gnarled Pine
Taoist Hermit

An old blind man slowly strummed a zither in a tavern at nighttime, a mournful tune for a mournful time. It had been quite a few years since I had parted from Happy Willow. Now I sought him out on hearing word of his troubles. Just as I had reversed my direction in life, he likewise did so—in the opposite direction. Had I neglected my bond with him? How had he strayed so far from the right path? These were my questions as I entered the tavern.

Happy Willow slept, drunk, with his head resting on a table. With my staff I struck the table and he awoke. His eyes were bloodshot and his hair was a mess. I spoke to him to understand his lot, and he relayed the following story.

"I took up my official post and life was good. I had all I wanted or ever could. Fruit Fruit and I shared laughter and life, but I took for granted my devoted wife. It began simply enough drinking with friends, but grew into something much worse in the end. After a night of gambling and wine, I committed against Fruit Fruit an offensive crime. As I walked home, stumbling along, I heard a lady of pleasure singing a song. I knew better than to do what I did. If only I could undo what from Fruit Fruit I hid. I entered this very tavern to that siren's song, and I greeted the woman with whom I did wrong. I woke the next day and hurried on home, dragging my guilt like a yoke of stone. Out of shame I should have stopped myself from repeating what I'd done, but I compounded my guilt by continuing on. I drank night after night and excused my sins by telling myself that I had already fallen within. I continued to spiral until Fruit Fruit came to know of my wanton ways. I'd fallen far from my better days. I shamed myself, for greed of self. I chose lust and betrayed her trust. She left my life, and from then on I have dwelled on my deviation from right. Mad I've become in my mind. I yearn to go back to atone for my crimes. But no one can uncast once-thrown dice. I gambled my morals and wife away to vice. It's hard to face the present while my mind lives in the past. I'm off to find peace, for the only escape I seek is eternal sleep."

Happy Willow then ran from the tavern, pushing me down as I tried to stop him. I could not find him once I gathered my feet and stepped outside. The slow, mournful strum of the zither carried on into the night.

Zhong Kui

I, Zhong Kui, the conscience of this tale, will intervene and finish this chapter. For when Happy Willow ran from Gnarled Pine's sight he entered my realm - read on for his plight.

"Welcome to hell, Happy Willow. Haven't we met before?" said Zhong Kui. "I know why you came—the same reason as did I. You took the selfish way out—by suicide. Oh, it must have been harsh to have been frozen to death, but all dying is over once you lose breath. Let me recall for you that day you did yourself in—yes, you escaped life, but to hell you came for that final sin. You drank at a tavern, becoming drunk once more, to build up the nerve for what you had in store. You hiked up the same mountain you did as a child, searching for escape as your mind ran wild. Then you stripped the clothes from your back, wrapped yourself around a pine tree, and waited for nature to act. The ice storm that day brought frozen sheets of rain, building layer upon layer on your skin. Slowly, with shivering pain, your body gave in, and now you stand here before me once again.

"Now, as before, will you join my side and fight to rid the world of evil? See, I only choose good souls that have done bad deeds. For with service, and in due time, I shall set your soul free. You shall be granted rebirth to earth once again, for wheels of life do spin and spin. Be wiser in your next life. But for now, be my soldier and pay your price. Earn good karma in my service, and set wrongs right. That is my offer. That is my oath."

Happy Willow replied, "I accept your offer and honor your oath. So is my sentence, so is my service. I'll work to cleanse my karma by fighting to earn it. That is my pledge. That is my oath. Demons and ghost fear it, for it's no drunken boast."

83

Chapter Thirteen

Stephen
Author & Artist

The year was 1998. The stone statue carving of Guan Yin was magnificent. I, Stephen, the author and artist of this tale, was at Longmen Caves near Luoyang, China. Longmen Caves is a series of man-made caves carved from a hillside along the Yi River. There are over two thousand caves containing thousands of Buddhist images. The main attractions of the area are the very large statues surrounding a large Guan Yin statue that serves as the focal point. I had traveled to China because of my strong interest in Chinese art, history, and culture. I chose the location of Luoyang primarily based on my interest in visiting the Shaolin Temple of the famed martial art (kung fu) experts of the Shaolin monks. The "Stephen" seal that you see in this book was carved by an artist who made seals for visitors. I wrote my name on a piece of paper and pronounced it for him so he could translate it into Chinese. I chose a stone with a monkey on top, as my birth year, 1968, was the year of the monkey.

My love for Chinese culture began with my interest in Chinese paintings. Also, I studied Chinese history and culture at The Ohio State University. Han culture began around the Yellow River and Yangtze River basins thousands of years ago. After visiting the capital city, Beijing, I traveled by train to the ancient capital of Luoyang on my quest to visit the Shaolin Temple.

I took a tourist van to the temple in the Song Mountains, and I loved seeing the countryside and people. Although the mountain scenery was breathtaking, our ascent was a bit frightening as the winding road up the mountain had no guard rails. My mind could not help but conjure up the image of the van plunging over the side of the mountain. I prayed that the steering column would not snap.

Outside the temple I found many vendors selling martial arts weapons to tourists. I had my picture taken several times in front of the temple and then proceeded inside to the courtyard grounds. As I toured the temple and read placards of historical interest, I came across one in front of a large stone. The sign said that this stone had imprinted on it the shadow of an Indian monk known as Damo. The legend goes that he meditated for nine years near the stone and that because of the length of time and the intensity of his meditation, his shadow image was left on the stone. As I continued to peruse the grounds of the temple, I noticed an old man in a white robe with a blue sash following me as I walked and stopping as I stopped. He had a long white beard and hair tied in a topknot; long white eyebrows; straight, upright posture; and a distinguished look. Also, he carried a walking staff. I thought perhaps he was some sort of character actor with whom tourists took pictures. After about four hours at the temple, I got back in the van and took the long, winding, scenic trip back to my hotel room in Luoyang.

The next day I set off to explore the city and countryside. I found a walking path on a nearby mountain and decided it would be fun to climb. After about half an hour, I came to a clearing with a small pond. At the

86

edge of the pond sat the same old man I'd seen at the Shaolin Temple. He was fishing, using his staff as a rod, with a line that led into the water. I strolled past, and in a mood to try out my Chinese, I said, "Ni hao," meaning hello. He replied in English without looking back, "Good morning, Happy Willow." I was surprised that he replied and that he spoke English.

"Pardon me. You speak English?" I asked.

He said, "I speak many tongues, for I find it very healthy to exercise my lungs."

"What did you mean by 'Happy Willow'?" I asked.

He replied, "I addressed you as who you were, not who you are. I knew you would return according to the stars. I can detect old souls of long ago. While flesh and bones rot and decay, the soul or mind carries on seeking the way. Your interests of your former self unknowingly brought you back this way. Inside your mind are unsettled longings that guide you this very day. You have transformed, my dear young cicada, but here have I stayed and patiently waited."

I was intrigued by the story he told, listening to how by stars he tracked my soul. For this tale, which you've read, is what that very day he said. He introduced himself as Gnarled Pine.

Gnarled Pine said, "I waited all these years to bring your soul's mind closer and to relay a message. I could think of no one better in whom to invest it. That day of death when you froze to the pine, you scribbled in snow your last peace of mind...

Fruit Fruit, I let you down,
I shed tears here on snowy ground.
Regret has ripped away at my heart,
Please forgive me after I part.

87

I led myself astray,
I lost sight of the promises I made.
We cannot return to former times,
But with forgiveness pardon my crimes.
Forgive me,
Forgive me,
Forgive me.

"That poem went undiscovered, but by one. For it was erased by blowing winds and warming sun. I know that poem because that very wind blew past my ears, and imparted upon me the words you had written there. To Fruit Fruit I passed on the poem, and with forgiveness she had one of her own…

I forgive you, once-husband of mine,
Our love is not lost to time.
It will always lie nestled in our hearts,
Even when from life we part.
We shared laughter and happiness,
With pain and sadness,
But the soul always has the morrow,
So face it with my forgiveness and freedom from sorrow.

"You see, Stephen," Gnarled Pine said, "our wheels of life have spun in opposite directions, and I have waited here for you in prayerful reflection."

I was numb and in doubt about what I heard. How could this be?

Suddenly his fishing line gave a tug, and he pulled a large, brown carp ashore. Holding the fish flapping in his hand, he said, "A man named Damo once told me a message that changed my fate, and in my mind I've kept it safe. Now I pass it on to you today so that this time you may follow the way."

In life, you and I are like this gasping fish;
The fish seeks air for his lungs,
In life we seek answers of what lies beyond.
Like the fish, we suffer in our search.
Like the fish we die to find truth.
For the answers we seek lie beyond this pond.
When our eyes lose sight, we see anew.
When faith supplants fear, who cares of death?
Such will be your own enlightenment.
Such is the way of life and death.

Gnarled Pine then tossed the fish back into the pond. The carp landed with a thud and water splashed onto my face. Suddenly the carp jumped up from the pond and tried to catch a passing cicada, but luckily it escaped safely to a nearby lotus leaf. A full moon lit the scene. Gnarled Pine noted that reincarnation could be avoided under the guise of enlightenment. "Seek the way," he said, "as the cicada sought the protection of the lotus."

Later I would learn through the scrolls that he gave me that the lotus was an analogy to the way. The lotus in Buddhism is symbolic of a person and their path to enlightenment. The lotus starts out deep in a pond and rises through the mud and muck of this world. Then upon breaking the surface of the pond, it blossoms into a beautiful flower. The flower represents the purity that one can obtain by following the right way to transcend the bonds of this world and break the cycle of birth, death, and rebirth.

Gnarled Pine explained that through Damo he learned that it is not in a particular doctrine that salvation is found. "Tear up scripture and you're still the same. Realize your own Buddha nature and forget the self. But don't get caught up in belief of no self. You and I are the mystery in between. From whence existence came, we will return, but from there we never left. Meditate on this, and observe the precepts of rightful action, for this is the Tao of Life and Death."

89

Gnarled Pine rose to leave and searched with his hand for his staff. It was then that I realized that he was blind. I inquired about his sight, and he stated that his blindness was not due to old age but due to enlightenment. His faith and rightful actions had given him the ability to see without seeing. Also, he stated that his posture had straightened in accordance with ending his penance. Quiet Buffalo had written to him that when his back was straight, he would no longer fear his fate.

Gnarled Pine could have left this world long ago, but out of a sense of duty he stayed to relay the message of forgiveness from Fruit Fruit and to convey the message of Damo. It was the final good deed from a once-crooked pine to a once-happy willow.

Gnarled Pine then handed me a drinking gourd filled with the seals you see in this book and a satchel containing scrolls of the stories written here. But I could not help doubting the story he told—and he sensed it. He pulled the turtle seal from the gourd, affixed it to a piece of paper, and lit the paper on fire. The smoke rose in the air and obscured my vision. When the smoke cleared, I saw a turtle walking away down the hiking trail. That was our goodbye.

蟬逃生作圖

91

Afterword

I beseech you to listen to the quiet moments before sleep. At this time we are most true with our thoughts. The weight of our own mortality is examined. For once we don't awake to a glistening morn; judgment itself cannot be spurned. Live the now for the ever after, and face fate with fearless laughter. If not, then perhaps we'll meet on my terms; so I say, so be warned.

—Zhong Kui

93   Zhong Kui

Stephen Self Portrait

Made in the USA
San Bernardino, CA
13 February 2017